v2

Amra

n19

Amra (of which this is volume 2 number 19 for February
1962) is published at Box
9006 Rosslyn, Arlington 9,
Virginia. Price: 20¢ each, 2$
for 10 issues; or 2/- each, 14/-
for 10 issues in sterling areas
to our Sterling Great British
Agent, Alan Dodd, 77 Stanstead Rd.,
Hoddesdon, Herts., England. Amra
comes out aperiodically, and not as
often as we'd like at that. ©1962
by The Terminius, Owlswick, & Ft Mudge
Electrick St Railway Gazette; lithographed in the United States of
America; all rights reserved.

Staff:

Art Editor: Dan Adkins -- Northern Cal-
ifornia Horse Editor: Liz Løkke née
Warren aka Wilson -- Southern Califor-
nia Horse & Rustling Editor: Bjo
Trimble -- Editors in charge of the
Addressing System: Bill Evans &
Larry Breed -- Nomenclature Editor:
Marion Zimmer Bradley -- Editor
in charge of The Magazine of Fan-
tasy & Science Fiction: Avram
Davidson -- Editor in charge
of insulting our Ancient &
Venerable Multilith: Walter
Breen -- Comic Editors: Don
Thompson, Maggie Curtis, &
Larry Ivie.   #+#+#+#+#

BLUNDERS
        by Ye incomparably numerous editors

There are a number of notes on hand on <u>Amra</u> volume 2 number 18.
Dick Tierney said his recommendation of L Sprague de Camp's new novel
THE BRONZE GOD OF RHODES sounded so enthusiastic that he thinks he will
read the book if he can locate it. He especially enjoyed his description
of the fighting Gargantyoi.

Our comment: if he didn't write "A Plea", who in Ymir's name did?

Fritz Leiber says the first maps of Lankhmar & vicinity were
labored sketches by himself and Harry Fischer. Then came the excellent
one, with pyramidal mountains and monster-decor, by Martha McElroy
Fischer, who a little later did cartography in WW II. But this final
version by Jim Cawthorn is perfectly clear, perfectly proportioned, and
perfectly charming!

He likes the rounded planetary effect at the top with the background stars, even if it does refute the Lankhmar hollow-earth or "bub-
ble" theory. And he's sure the alternate spellings given a couple of the
names are well-established regional variants. One should remember that
it's about 400 miles from Lankhmar to Kvarch Nar and then all the dis-
tances come clear. True, the Land of the Eight Cities looks just a bit
like a Michigan or Wisconsin summer resort, but anyone who wanders
around the Great Forest under this delusion will most certainly get his
head snapped off.

He's learning more about Nehwon all the time now -- says Fritz --
for instance he can see now that they can have some pretty terrific
storms in the Inner Sea with a west wind. He's hung the map above his
desk and begun to dream. Specifically, he's finishing a tale about the
youth of the Mouser, even before he met Fafhrd, which will be submitted
to <u>Fantastic</u> shortly. It's set in that clump of trees east of the Lakes
of Pleea. . . . .

Bob Briney points out that a good bit of the review of THE DYING
EARTH was quasi-quoted.

And Bjo Trimble asks howcome if we include all those horsey editors
we don't got horses. She speaks as a country-raised gal, who has on
occasion "jumped" **without saddle or bridle**, injun style (sometimes without horse, if he changed his mind at the last moment). She even "rus-
tled" a whole horse for an afternoon, but her mother made her put him
back.

Well, we did have a horse -- Tam Pearce's
old grey mare. Unfortunately, she
was loaned to some friends to go
to Widdicombe Fair, and on
the way back, she
took sick
and
died
##

Three Hearts & Three Lions

Reviewed
by
Dick
Eney

I was driving down the street the other day, waiting for the filling of that niche in the domains of fantasy which had been vacated by the disappearance of de Camp and Pratt, when some of the editors of Amra drew my attention to the book version of Poul Anderson's THREE HEARTS & THREE LIONS.

I'm still waiting for that niche to be filled. And those of you who remember ol' Three of one and a quarter dozen of the other from its serial appearance in F&SF will be pretty disappointed in the newer version.

For those who didn't meet it the first time around, the tale is of one Holger Carlsen, who gets his skull creased by a bullet during a fight between the Danish underground and the Nazis and . . . wakes up in a medieval forest on the border of Middle Earth, next to a knight's charger carrying gear made to his measure. You can figure out what's happened -- this sort of change-by-concussion is almost as much a stock convention in adventure fantasy as is the rocketship in science-fiction. It becomes apparent rather soon that, whoever Holger may be in this world, he's somebody important enough for the forces of Chaos (Pharies, Trolls, Giants, and other Middle-World creatures) to be in great haste to kill him before he can find out his identity, retrieve a mysterous sword named Cortana, and thus become a force for Law (the Holy ((Roman)) Empire plus the Saracen kingdoms, if you haven't a map handy).

Nobody could imagine a writer like Poul Anderson flubbing so perfect a setup for adventure-fantasy. And he didn't. Moreover, to the obvious opportunities for adventure-fantasy was added just that right touch of madly scientific logic that was the making of the Harold Shea stories; the thermodynamic aspects of the dragon problem, for instance, and the state of metallurgy among a nation whose warriors couldn't touch iron. A thoroughly satisfying story, and -- being less cut than most F&SF serials -- neatly balanced and compacted.

Unhappily, it wasn't long enough for a hardcover book. I found out from Poul at the Seacon that he'd had to add episodes to bring it up to a decent length. And as for these interpolations . . . weeeeell . . . .

In padding the story, alas, I suspect Poul tripped not only over the obvious handicap of anyone whose hero is committed to defending medieval civilization against Faerie, but also over the obvious generic resemblance between 3&3 and THE MATHEMATICS OF MAGIC. That is, he added deliberate comedy to the interpolated sections; and, ghod help us, often slapstick comedy. The balk here, of course, is that Poul's vein is properly witty and humorous, not farcically comic (as those who recall the horrors of the Hoka series well know); so the effect is something less than might be desired when Holger plays the riddle-game with Balamorg the Giant and tries to win by ringing in Sick Jokes. ("What has four legs, weighs 800 pounds, and sings?" "Two 400 pound canaries." Yargh!)

A more awkward point -- and one made worse by the attempt at solution -- is this: Holger finds himself committed to fighting the hosts of Faerie and the Middle World, and all the legends Poul has to go on make such a decision ridiculous by logic. That is, from the first appearance of the people of Faerie, it's obvious that Holger has gotten into the fight on the wrong side; that what anybody with a lick of sense would naturally do, given a modern cultural orientation, would be to aid the speedy victory of the Middle World and abolish the medieval Empire. The Faerie folk are clearly shown as superior to the best Medievalism could offer in every important respect -- intelligence, level of culture, and lack of a class brutalized by toil -- and inferior in only two items -- personal strength and sensitivity to ultra-violet -- which technology could set right in jig time. The only instance of barbaric, savage evil -- a child sacrifice at a coven meeting -- is performed by humans.

There is one ineffectual attempt to make the Middle World folk out to be worse than humanity, on the ground of their moral callousness (on account of their lack of souls, remember?). As to the motivation for this effort, I suspect Poul realized that he'd made the tacit case for Faerie too strong and introduced this (it's one of the interpolated episodes) as a counterpoint. As to its sucess, however . . . well, after all, it depends on being able to convince us that the Middle World creature involved (a water-nixie named Rusel) is more callous than a human being could be. But to imagine anybody surpassing the recorded accomplishments of our own Inquisitions and Gestapos you'd have to be sicksicksick. Poul is not sick; thus his attempt to give some logical justification for Holger's course of action falls pretty flat. Not to add insult to injury or like that, but the attempt isn't really necessary anyway; I think we're all pretty well conditioned to accept that humans back humans, in adventure fantasy or elsewhere,

THREE HEARTS & THREE LIONS

when a clash with Aliens is involved.

Mind you, now, I've been deliberately picking out the weak features of this version. It should go without saying that much, even most, of the interpolated passages are as good as we expect Poul's stuff to be -- say, the episode of the Werewolf of Lourville, with its denounment in the best detective-story style. And there are a puckle of examples of his being witty rather than comical . . . my own best laugh, if you want to know, came when Duke Alfric -- mediating on the possibility that the world from which Holger came was the dream-source of Faerie's legends about the Emperor Napoleon and his paladins -- thoughtfully quoted a triplet from the Geste of the Brigadier Gerard. And the excellent original story still stands as framework on which the later passages were tacked. But damn, I wish those additions had all been up to the measure of their substructure!

###########

OLD KING KULL
(From "Honkings from Maw Goose")

Old King Kull
Had a sword quite dull,
        An' a sword quite dull had he,
So he called for his fire,
And he called for his forge
        And he called for his metalsmiths three.

Said the head smith: "Kull,
Your sword isn't dull --
        Try its temper and you will see."
So Old King Kull
Cleft the metalsmith's skull,
        And he said: "You're as right as can be!"

Dick Tierney###

Swackle: On Names
                by L Sprague de Camp
Names are the recurrent nightmare of the writer of any story in an exotic setting: past, future, or purely imaginary. Howard gave names to only two of his Picts: Zogar Sag (in "Beyond the Black River") & Gorm (in "The Hyborian Age"). The latter is properly an Old Norse name. Some real Pictish names are known from inscriptions (Scientific American, Nov '60, p 166): Resad, Spusscio, Canutulachama, Bliesblituth, Usconbuts, Uipoinamet, Uumpopula, & Doronauch Nerales. Try these on modern sight-reading readers! But they are no worse than the ancient Karians, who had names like Äāviädhüs, Khmivoskh, Ravussdeave, Sskhäeä, Yüvlâvuhssai, Khadhheh, Ääuladhe, Tosuvth, Svāokh, Lereüdânsa, etc.
                        Ogresden, Wallingford, Penna###

Remember, O artists: Project Art Show plans an exhibit at the 20th World Science Fiction, Labor Day weekend, 1962. For details on the exhibit, write for information from Bjo Trimble, 222 South Gramercy Place, Los Angeles 4. A $1.50 gets from her the Project Art Show bulletin. Membership in the Chicon itself; $2 to Box 4864, Chicago 80.
                                        ###

6

LITTLE MEN IN BIG BOOTS: A comparison of THE KING MUST DIE and THE
BRONZE GOD OF RHODES by Juanita Coulson

No less a recognized critic than Damon Knight has stated: "de Camp
is too wise to believe wholeheartedly in anything."* With this rather
left-handed compliment, this reviewer attacks the problem of analyzing
L Sprague de Camp's THE BRONZE GOD OF RHODES and comparing it with another work, with a bit easier soul. Though he is not dealing with a pre-
history hero, de Camp is handling much the same problem as Miss Renault
in THE KING MUST DIE; both are describing a physically small man's
struggle for sucess. Miss Renault's treatment has a haunting reality, a
reality almost chilling at times, drawing the reader into both her hero's dilemma and the very period of history which she treats. De Camp
writes a rollicking good story, amusing, exciting, and laced with as-
suredly authentic background -- and a story branded on each page with
the author's dry wit trademark.

In the end, de Camp's city of Rhodes and his hero Chares lack the
impact of reality of Renault's Troizen, Athens, Crete, and the hero-
brought-to-life that is her Theseus. One gets the feeling Mr de Camp
is never quite able to convince himself -- never quite able to reach
that all-necessary suspension of disbelief required of a writer of convincing heroic fiction. His worldiness shows.

Both heroes struggle for recognition, Chares to build his colossus
and Theseus to achieve his true kinghood. Both are small men and pain-
fully aware of the fact; both overcome numerous odds made more fearsome
by this same fact. But in the struggle, Chares emerges as a comic re-
lief hero, while the reader is drawn into Theseus' problems, sympath-
izes, and indeed seethes over the arrows of fate which strike the small
man.

Both books study the struggle to achieve a dream. De Camp lays the
tale of the sculptor Chares, returning to his beloved Rhodes after a
period of study abroad, first conceiving a plan of building a greater
statue than any yet known; he is drawn into the battle of Rhodes, where-
in Rhodes held out sucessfully against the beseiger, Demetrious Antigo-
nou, makes several historically interesting and fictionally entertaining side ventures into pockets of the post-Alexandrian world and finally succeeds in his dream. Miss Renault recounts in non-mythical terms
the rise of Theseus from son of the myrtle grove to the discovery of
his paternity in Athens, his captivity in Crete as a bull-vaulter, and
his final successful overthrow of the "minotaur" -- the king must, indeed, die.

Not only are the motives of these heroes for striving different,
but also their personal attitudes. Chares, though moved by a vision of
Apollo, is still the sophisticated agnostic who does not quite believe
in his own motives: "Do you want to know the real reason I erected that
statue? It wasn't money . . . nor was it an excess of piety, though I
am a good conventional worshipper of the Bright One. The reason is that
I'm a small man, so I have always wanted to be remembered for building
the largest thing of its kind." (p 399, BRONZE GOD OF RHODES.) But when

* IN SEARCH OF WONDER (Advent: Publishers, Chicago) p 13)

Theseus, after the tragic death of his father, is in truth a king, he accepts the mood of the age, when man seemed much closer to the life-death cycle of all nature: "We were both in Poseidon's hand; it was for him to chose. Man born of woman cannot outrun his fate." (p 366, THE KING MUST DIE.) It is the fatalistic primitive contrasted with the sophisticate, even as the two novels are separated chronologically.

In this difference, it seems both authors are valid. However, it is one thing to try to capture the tenor of a time, and another to convince the reader that this exists, here, in print. In this wise, de Camp may well be at a greater disadvantage because the time he treats is so much closer in mood and motive to our own era than is the misty historical dawn of THE KING MUST DIE. Certainly, there is quite a difference in the reality of the two novels.

Theseus is much as the reader would conceive the hero-in-the-making, quite real, very human, and his world almost frighteningly vivid, dark horrors lurking around every twist, the all-pervading moira, and in short the feel, convincing, that This Is What It Was Like.

De Camp's Rhodes, and Alexandria, and Mediterranean are undoubtedly authentic and quite accurate, and his people highly entertaining. But with no exceptions, one might change names, pick up the characters bodily and put them down on an alien planet as members of Viagens Interplanetarias. They are charming people, or rogueish, or witty, but they are de Camp people, and as such they have no more the feel of the fourth century BC Mediterranean than Krishnans would.

In another matter Miss Renault scores a significant point. Chares, de Camp's hero, is presented as a small man, but his reactions are those that a large man might imagine a small man to have. (This writer will be forgiven if she suspects that Mr de Camp used as his model for Chares a certain well-known science-fiction fan turned pro, also of small stature, noted for bombast of the amusing sort.) Describing the actions of a small man can be done, but in this particular case it was not convincing. Part of the difficulty lies in the first person narration. De Camp has Chares spout off at great pompous length before a group of elders, and amusingly so for the reader, but without Chares at any point suspecting the elders' lack of interest; it should be pointed out that the hero is no callow youth -- in his twenties, he shades Theseus by better than five years -- but shows the social astuteness of a nine-year-old by contrast. De Camp seems to be laughing at his hero. If he had been writing as a narrator rather than a personal interpreter the snickering would not be quite so obvious. Chares is not quite a puppet, but his own interpretations of his actions ring false again and again throughout the book.

One suspects that a feminine writer reared in a Western culture has an unfair advantage in writing of a hero of small stature (further borne out by the example of another sucessful feminine writer who deals frequently and well with the problems of small, down-trodden heroes: Andre Norton). The Western culture female is trained to use her mind and pointed at a career and then told or otherwise persuaded abruptly that she is forever to be inferior physically. The outward result of such a shock, as de Camp has pictured so amusingly, is sometimes bom-

bast and unbearable strutting. The _inward_ result, shown much more vividly by Miss Renault, is deep bitterness and a great development of intelligence and cunning. The small bombast of such talent as given Chares
might _play_ the strut, but far more often bitter calculation would lie
behind the method -- calculation that would certainly show in a first
person narration. Not until fairly late in the book does Chares begin
to show glimmerings of this cunning, this acceptance of his size and
plotting to circumvent it; this would be believable if he were a young
adolescent, but this is a grown man in an era when people had to mature
early in order to mature at all.

Theseus is small and learns to compensate by wrestling tricks and
by using his quick mind to leap ahead of others, and to swallow insults:
"If I could not outgrow them, I must prove myself some other way . . .
These contests I won, having more at stake than the others, though I
never said so." (p 22, THE KING MUST DIE.) He is younger still than de
Camp's Chares, but he has early learned the bitter lesson of the small
by biting off retort and scheming ahead, while Chares goes blithely
ahead butting his head into older and wiser ones until quite late in
his career.

Bluntly, it is unconvincing in the extreme.

Returning to the matter of reality, of _feel_, of atmosphere, this
writer finds things a bit harder to divide, to state points for one
author or the other. A sense of humor, which de Camp liberally demon-
strates, is certainly no crime; if anything, Miss Renault suffers from
having too little. But then the period she treats was not one noted for
the lightness of its humor -- death delt in a crude manner was subject
for humor, and is now and then mentioned. By contrast, the Alexandrians,
Rhodians, or Interplanetarians-transplanted that populate THE BRONZE
GOD OF RHODES have a blunt, good-natured humor that appeals in contem-
porary terms; quite possibly humor is eternal, but the framing of the
conversations jolts the reader out of the chronological mood of the
story. Again, they are good jokes, but they are stamped "de Camp" from
straight line to punch. Even where a joke is not involved, the typically
de Campian dialogue jars in a tale of post-Alexandrian affairs -- or
possibly this is because the reader so rarely encounters, for example,
military instructions of this era in just exactly this sort of language:
"Another thing to remember is to use the standard words of command.
When you mean 'shoot', say 'shoot', not 'give the polluted bastards one
in the guts.'" (p 77, THE BRONZE GOD OF RHODES.) What is going on, of
course, is a translation of what the people sounded like to themselves,
rather than identifying the period by using deliberately archaic speech,
but what one is used to is tossed aside reluctantly. As humor, it is
good -- as swashbuckle, it is unnerving.

This difference in feel runs through the entire novel. When de
Camp describes the hero's search for the proper river channel entrance,
one has the distinct impression de Camp knows what he's talking about,
and indeed has undoubtedly _seen_ the place, but the description smacks
of a 20th Century tourist. On the other hand, in THE KING MUST DIE, the
maze of the minotaur, still existing and possibly toured by the author,
ceases to be a modern ruin and becomes _real_, populated, smelling of
fresh earth, unmusty -- transporting the reader in time emotionally

until he is not merely entertained by the book but grabbed, moved, and made just a little part of a world full of the Mother, the Minotaur, and the Earth Shaker.

The themes of the two books are basically similar -- the search for meaning, for success, the striving to conquer a task despite incredible obstacles, but the conclusions drawn are quite different. In the end, Chares builds his statue, and is somewhat sad in that he can never surpass himself in this particular end; but he has fame and plans, and in a small way (no pun) is happy. In THE KING MUST DIE, when the king dies, as he inevitably must, it does nothing but point the way for Theseus, caught up in the truth of life for all kings. It is important to understand that Theseus is neither particularly disturbed nor surprised by his fate; he not only has a fatalistic, hands-of-the-gods attitude, but the entire unfolding of the book, of his life and the life of the era, has prepared the way for this fatalism, this acceptance of the unending cycle: "It is the bloodletting that calls down power. It is the consenting, Theseus. The readiness is all." -- "She looked at me puzzled; I thought it was my Hellene speech, and said again, 'The laws of battle?' She raised her brows and answered, 'The law is that the King must die.' . . . I knew him at once, because he was alone."

Miss Renault's theme is consistent, and compelling -- readiness, acceptance, and -- the king must die. One of your editors has truthfully commented that it is a magnificently titled book, with every word, even the article, a necessary part of its importance. Theseus, as the kings who died before him, must "go consenting" -- this is the truth, and the very effective feel of the novel, and it gives THE KING MUST DIE the conclusive points.

We each have our moira -- authors too?

################

Swackle: ON CHARIOT OPERAS R E Briney

The Italian spectacle-makers, who have for a couple of years specialized in making movies for people who like men, have finally come up with a movie for people who like women: THE WARRIOR EMPRESS, with Tina Louise in the title rôle (playing a character who is, of course, neither a warrior nor an empress . .). The usual magnificent sets, inane plot, and shoddy editing; plus some acting which is better than the average for such films, and good dubbing in the non-English-speaking parts. And the advantage of a hero -- played by Kerwin (Sinbad-Gulliver) Mathews -- who can register at least the simpler emotions convincingly, move without rippling like a flag in the wind, and play a love scene without visible embarassment, thus affording a significant improvement over the stone-faced Reeves-Forest type. The film has the usual amount of swordplay, the usual sea battle, and just a touch of fantasy (in a scene which has nothing to do with the plot, and makes very little sense); and even a touch of Lesbianism, which is perhaps to be expected, since the heroine is the poetess Sappho, and the locale the island of Lesbos. Department of Mathematics, 2-174, MIT, Cambridge 39, Mass. ###

A GOLDEN SHEEPSKIN IN THE FORM OF A SCROLL: JASON -- by Henry Treece
reviewed by Jim Cawthorn

"The frozen creature in the chair did not answer me with
his voice or hands. But his fear-crazed eyes swung to
left and to right. I looked and saw the reason for his
terror. On either side of him, squatting on their haunches,
were the women..... white faces full of eyes, large
black Cretan eyes, that saw everything and saw nothing
..... and in each woman's lap rested a little silver
sickle."

So Jason of the Argonauts, raised in the mascu-
line society of the Horse-herders, first encounters
the dark aftermath of their annual visit to the Village
of the Women; always, one man must remain to "give The
Mother her due." And for the remainder of his life this
experience in his seventeenth year instils in him a
deadly fear of the power and cruelty of women, under-
lying all the scheming, adventuring, killing, and plun-
dering that surrounds his quest for the Golden Fleece.

Henry Treece brings the world of the Argonauts
vividly to life -- the interminable plotting of petty
kings, the haphazard wars dominated by egocentric cham-
pions, the casual brutality and bawdy humor that applied
itself impartially to spearmen and the daughters of
princes, and most of all the overpowering, bloody aura of terror and
superstition surrounding the cult of The Mother. The story follows
fairly closely the familiar twists and turns of the
legend, but the interpretation of motive differs; the
magical element, too, is largely rationalized; it is
Treece's particular gift to be able to do this without destroying the atmosphere of supernatural doom
that pervades so much of the action.

From his entry into Iolcos to fulfil his
mother's dream of slaying the usurper, King
Pelias, to his own eventual kingship and disas-
trous involvement with Creon, conqueror of
Mycenae, Jason's fate is determined almost
wholly by the ambitions of others. Seen through
the eyes of a poet-novelist, the others are a
superb cast of characters, notably Heracles, mon-
strously strong, prone to bouts of madness and
perversion in which he believes himself to be possessed by The Mother; lithe Atalanta, who as repre-
sentative of the Virgin Moon-Goddess shows little
sense of vocation; blonde, long-legged Hypsipyle,
Queen of the High Gate and Jason's only real love; and
dark Medea the snake-priestess, embodiment of the
power which he dreads. Jason himself, narrating the
tale of his earlier days, emerges as a living personal-
ity knowing triumph and defeat, reckless courage, and

numbing fear.

In short, I recommend this book to fantasy-lovers and readers of straight historical novels alike; those already familiar with Treece's series set in Celtic Britain will, I think, find him equally at home on the wine-dark sea.

WEARINESS OF WAR

(In 1064 AD, King Harald Hardrede of Norway and King Svein Ulfsson of Denmark met to see if their long struggle for the Danish crown could be settled. Both brought great armies. None knew if the truce would end in peace being made, or in a battle which would resume the destructive war. It was the former which happened -- Harald abdicated his claims -- perhaps, in part, because of this verse, whose composer is unknown but which was heard in both camps.)

Many folk their mouths use
at meeting, in each army;
haughtiness breeds hatred
in hosts of Dane and Norseman.
None will wish to nod
his neck unto another;
and the kings are angry,
egging on the trouble.

Warlike royal wills
give warning of ill tidings;
men who'd act as makepeace
measure into scalepans.
Fearlessly and freely
folk should say their wishes:
evil is this hour
if enemies go homeward.

---(tr. from the ON. by
Poul Anderson)

HYBORIANS BE SEATED

by

Ray Capella

SPLATT! ! SPLATT! !

The young bront slaps his long tail twice, into the lagoon's muddy waters.

"I'm sick of it, I tell you," he grumbles, great neck arched in anger, "It's time for a showdown! And with our allies' we'll beat them into the lava sea!"

The older brontosaurus swivels his rounded head to look at him with heavy-lidded eyes: "All allosauri got teeth, son. And friends, too. Between them and us we make up most of dinosaurkind. Gonna jeopardize it with war."

"Jeopardize dinokind? Balderdash!" scoffs the young bront. "A short scrimmage and they'll quit. We're larger, heavier. Maybe not as cunning, but wiser. And many of us are tired of being insulted and shamed by them. They've been getting away with murder -- and laughing at us! It's time we fought! Have you no pride?"

"Pride! Pride and shame and ridicule and fighting!" Old bront rumbles deep within the spaces of his huge stomach. He belches ponderously and some flying creatures are checked in midflight as they pass him, dropping to the water. "That for your petty emotions! On such things you'd base a war of annihilation?"

"Until we find a species better worth preserving," he adds with heavy scarcasm, "We should preserve dinokind no matter what. Is one group's pride or principle worth the price of extinction? For all groups? I think not....no, I think not.."

The old one sinks his head into the mud, peering for another mouthful. The young brontosaurus lumbers away with disdain.

"Words, words," he roars, neck looped over one shoulder as he looks back. "Extinction! You elders are all pessimists. Words won't hold you when it gets crowded around here, and food gets scarce. Then you'll sing a different tune...!"

("Ha! I'd show those who'd live by the sword -- I'd drop the Bomb and I'd force Peace right down their bloodthirsty throats!"

Deacon Mushrat
THE POGO PAPERS
1952)

Gentlemen, be seated. Sir -- you in the back with the double-handled sword -- would you mind? Thank you. Don't glare, lady, I'm a Hyborian too . . . By taste, if not by birth.

We're here to look at the field with less partiality, Hyborians or not. There were other storytellers, you know. And many deserve an honored place within our walls.

Writers like to eat, more often than not. Some of those in the past tinged their stories with pseudo-science to sell to magazines that were then publishing the stuff, thus giving their fantasy yarns a certain ambiguous status in the field. But if they evoked a mood more of the fantastic than s-f, and held the fire of sorcery and terror to temper the adventure, I think they should be mentioned here.

Abe Merritt, in most cases, wrote fantasy. His stories were based on a seemingly boundless knowledge of folklore, or extrapolated legend. His s-f, if any, is and will remain questionable for a hell of a long time.

Whether or not he wrote series about his heroes is of no consequence; he belongs. And strangely enough, I've rarely heard him mentioned in Amra.

No reader of Merritt will ever forget Leif Langdon, the brooding lead figure in THE DWELLERS IN THE MIRAGE. He stands as the "Conan" of Merritt's heroes.

And Merritt had a "John Carter" too, in the protagonist of his classic SHIP OF ISHTAR. Matter of fact, Kenton was considerably more real than John Carter. Burroughs had a habit of waving his characters' code of honor like a bloody flag, until one got sick of their cardboard qualities. Merritt's people lived their principles wordlessly, so to speak. It's the same difference as you might find in two of the current movie spectaculars, for instance, the unadulterated cornball flagwaving of "The Alamo" and the artful handling of a similar struggle for principles in "Spartacus".

Merritt was a word-weaver, a painter of minute detail and description, in his effort to give his stories beauty and authenticity, but this never got in the way of his action, for his plots moved, and his battles would satisfy the most bloodthirsty Howard fan. And he had exquisite taste in the handling of his ideas. Where Burroughs and maybe Kline might milk their formulas to the point of idiocy, Merritt treated his wholly within the confines of whatever length the ideas' development required. This usually came to a novel, or an introductory novelette followed by a novel. The Merritt fan might thirst for more of Kenton's adventures with the SHIP OF ISHTAR, but that one novel will haunt him as long as he can remember.

Who knows -- Burroughs' Mars series might've been termed "classic" by fantasy aficionados, too, if the collection had been limited to three books.

Like the others, of course, Merritt had his formulas, too. His theme was the old, lost-race, ancient-gods bit. And he had a sort of stock cast of characters: Hero, Heroine, and Villainess who competed in beauty and sorcery, a behind-the-scenes Villain (or Creature), and his Powerful Priest-Tool. And the author seemed to have a fixation for a second-lead character which I found in at least three of his novels: the mighty dwarf, short but of powerful proportions, who was sometimes one the "good" side, sometimes on the "bad". All enacted their turbulent drama against an eerie setting.

14

And what settings they were! The deck of a fairy ship, the misty bottom of a mirage, the huge, shining caverns of the land beneath the Moon Pool! Furthermore, the characters developed such personalities within their surroundings that they always remained distinct in comparison with similar groups in other novels.

The old fantasy fan will know which of Merritt's yarns I've considered to be Sword-and-Sorcery from what I've said so far: THE SHIP OF ISHTAR, THE CONQUEST OF THE MOON POOL, and THE DWELLERS IN THE MIRAGE. Not having read its sequel, I don't know if FACE IN THE ABYSS would have evolved into the same category. I do know that for weird writing, FACE IN THE ABYSS introduced some of what might be the strangest of the author's imaginings.

With the latter, Merritt's style was subtly -- changed. His creatures and gods in the previously mentioned stories (the little people, the Kraken in DWELLERS, Ishtar and the gods in SHIP, and the terrifying Dweller in MOON POOL, etc.) came alive in detail and colorful mood. But in FACE IN THE ABYSS, the description was violently expressionistic, yet nonetheless vivid. For me it was nightmarish -- yet real.

THE METAL MONSTER was the only Merrittale that bogged down. From fannish comments and criticisms I've found this seems to be general opinion. The story moved from one tremendous descriptive step to another, as if the author were trying to pen the movements in some fantastic symphony. For some reason, the grandeur in each scene brings Sibelius' "Finlandia" to mind, though I heard this piece long after having read the novel. In any case, so much of the tale was taken up by this that characterization and plot seemed limited to the very beginning and conclusion of the narrative.

Merritt wrote THE METAL MONSTER after CONQUEST OF THE MOON POOL, and linked sword-and-sorcery to his attempt at horror -- the character-narrator was the same. Aside from this, there was little connection between the two novels. A similar **relationship** came out in two of his best pieces of modern horror -- BURN, WITCH, BURN and CREEP, SHADOW. These were two of his later works, and though not in the same category of fantasy-adventure as SHIP OF ISHTAR, etc., no horror story fan'll deny them a place of honor in that field.

There were more . . . the short fantasy pieces at which Mr Merritt excelled, the suspenseful mystery novel, SEVEN FOOTPRINTS TO SATAN . . But, as I'm trying to keep this for the sword-and-sorcery reader it'll suffice to mention them in passing. I will assert, however, that I thought SATAN more frightening than Rohmer's FU MANCHU and Howard's SKULL-FACE put together.

Aside from the latter comparison, I find Howard and Merritt on the same level. Some might say the "Lord of Fantasy" (as the old fantasy crowd used to call him) was more literary, but I'd say this was confusing skill for style. Way I see it -- place a detailed, beautiful oil behind a grim, primitive statuette of equal aesthetic value and you'll have my estimation from Merritt to Howard.

Now gentlemen, please lower the spear-points as you pass through the door -- those drapes were filch— uh, donated by a very rich

Nemedian count. I hope the attendance will be as good next time around
-- there were others, you -- please, sir! With the double-handled sword
-- would you be careful with that thing? Somebody give the other gen-
tleman a hand, will you -- Oh, is he? Well, maybe we can get another
member by the next meeting . . . . .

DE CAMP'S PAGE

by L Sprague de Camp
(You expected maybe Avram Davidson?)

DEPARTMENT OF ADDENDA TO THE EXEGESIS:
ALTAKU, WELL OF -- in QC, a well in the Oasis of Aphala; from
Altaqu or Eltekeh, a place in ancient Judah, about 12 miles WNW of
Jerusalem, where the Assyrians of King Sennacherib defeated the Egypt-
ians in 700 BC.
GEBAL -- possibly from the town of that name in Lebanon -- also
spelled Jebeil and Jubayl, classical Byblos, Phoenician Gubla.
SHIRKI -- possibly (though this is far-fetched) from Sirki, the
original Assyrian name of a town at the confluence of the Euphrates &
Khabur rivers, later called Phaliga, Circesium, and Buseira or
Bessireh.
THUGRA -- more likely from the Thugra Gorge near Petra, in Jordan.
This supposition is strengthened by the fact of Howard's extensive
knowledge of the territories in the Middle East that were fought over
in the Crusades, apparently one of Robert E Howard's favorite subjects
for reading.

DEPARTMENT OF CHRONOGRAPHY:
Apropos the Boardman-Davidson discussion of Hyborian timekeeping:
"The Hour of the Dragon" is derived from the Chinese system of hours,
which divides the mean solar day into 12ths (not 24ths as with us). The
first shï or double-hour runs from 2300 to 0100 (armed services time)
thus straddling midnight; the 2nd, 0100 to 0300, etc. The names are the
hours of the Rat, Ox, Tiger, Hare, Dragon, Snake, Horse, Sheep, Monkey,
Cock, Dog, and Boar, in that order. Hence the Hour of the Dragon, 0700
--0900, could be translated simply "breakfasttime". Ref.: HEAVENLY
CLOCKWORK, by Needham, Wang Ling, & Price (Camb., 1960), a work on
medieval Chinese horology (which has nothing to do with sex).

DEPARTMENT OF THE TIMES:
I quote:
"Athens, April 12 -- An ancient Hall of Hades, described by Homer
as the gateway to the underworld abode of the dead, has been found
by archeologists in Epirus, northwestern Greece.
"The discovery was made near the banks of the Acheron River, which
in ancient mythology was believed to have conveyed the souls of the
dead to the lower world...
"Soltirios Dakaris, head of the Greek archeological service in
Epirus, announced that he had identified such a hall [of Hades] in a
massive rectilinear structure, 200 by 145 feet, which dates from the
third century BC.
"He said it was likely that the structure, known as a Necroman-
teion, or Oracle of the Dead, was built on the site of an earlier
structure that Homer himself might have visited...where the Kokytus
River flows into the Acheron..." New York Times, 23 April 61, p 41.

DEPARTMENT OF ARTWORK & REPRODUCTION:
For the Hyborian portfolio, why not some of the pix of Jean A D
Ingres (French, 1780- 1867), the leading portrayer of curly-pubic-
haired classical-mythical heroes?

###########

A SCROLL OF SIRRUSH HIDE AND PAPYRUS: THE DRAGON OF THE ISHTAR GATE
G H Scithers reviewing   a book by L Sprague de Camp

"The time was before dawn on the morning of the third day of the month Nisanu, in the twentieth year of the reign of Xerxes -- the Great King, the King of All Kings, the king of the Persians and the Medes, the king of the wide world, the son of Darius, the chief of the Achaemenid clan. The place was a chamber of the west side of the small palace of Darius at Persepolis, in the rugged mountains of Parsa."*

So begins L Sprague de Camp's latest historical novel, THE DRAGON OF THE ISHTAR GATE. The principal characters are soon introduced. First there are King Xerxes himself and his wizard Ostanas; this wizard is planning an elixir for the king, but lacks three ingredients: the ear of a king, the blood of a dragon, and the heart of a hero.

The scene shifts swiftly, to the home of Myron Perseôs, a broad-shouldered Greek from Miletos who makes his living as a tutor of the the Persian nobility. Myron is besought by the doting mother of a for-mer pupil to save her son from execution that dawn. Tears and bribes move Myron not, untill the lady tries another means, and says:

"'If you must have logic, consider this, good my sir. When one of your former pupils comes to a bad end, it reflects upon your teaching. You claim to impart wisdom; yet events give your words the lie. Had Bessas possessed wisdom, he would not now face a mean and agonizing death.'

"Myron drew a deep breath as his face cleared. 'Your arguments are irrefutable, lady. I will do what I can.'"

What he can is most sucessful -- he persuades Xerxes to pardon the former pupil, Bessas, provided that Bessas go and capture a sirrush, a fabulous, dragon-like beast, whose likeness is to be found on the Ishtar Gate in Babylon.** Xerxes also demands that Bessas procure the ear of a king. Ostanas has persuaded Xerxes that whoever can bring back these two ingredients will certainly be an authentic hero, so the less said about the third ingredient in advance . . . . .

Rather to his own surprise, Myron persuades the King to let him go on the expedition too -- "For Myron Perseôs was a collector of facts, as other men collected concubines or horses or gold. Sometimes he tempor-arily forgot them, as does a squirrel the nuts it has buried. But the facts were all there, locked away in his squarish skull, waiting for some reminder to call them forth. He secretly hoped that some day these facts would fall into a pattern -- a pattern that should give a profound new insight into the nature of things and place his name with those of Thales and Herakleitos among the great lovers of wisdom. Although it had never occurred, and Myron sometimes feared he was simply not clever

---

* All quotes are from THE DRAGON OF THE ISHTAR GATE.

** The sirrush is discussed at length in chapter 9 of Willy Ley's THE LUNGFISH, THE DODO, AND THE UNICORN; in fact, the chapter title is the source of the title of Sprague's book.

enough to build a noble edifice of thought from his myriad bricks of fact, he never completely gave up hope."

All in all, Myron is a very typical de Camp sort of hero, life sized but no more than that, full of ideas, doubting everything in sight including particularly his own abilities, and logical as only a Classical Greek can be. As Bessas says to Myron, "'It is well that you're not going on this journey. Else, when some savage chieftain is making up his mind whether to chop our heads off, you would correct his speech and get us slain for sure.'"

So too, the story of their adventures -- for Myron does go on the expedition -- would be a typical de Camp story but for Bessas the Bactrian, who the reader meets on the point of being impaled, and is barely rescued by Myron. Most of the subsequent rescuing is the other way around, however.

"Bessas son of Phraates towered over all the rest. [He] was a heavy-featured man, six and a half feet tall and massively muscled. Under a disordered mop of black hair were a broad forehead, heavy black brows, deep-set brown eyes, wide cheekbones, a long nose (which had been straight until a sword cut had put a kink in it), and full lips. A short beard masked his massive jaw. But for the pocks that marked his face, he would have been handsome in a rugged, somber way.

"Although but thirty, Bessas bore the scars of a veteran. One ran from the left temple down into the beard, another across the right cheek, and others were to be seen on neck and arms and running through the mat of curly black fur that covered his chest."

In action, he is just as impressive: "'There is no doubt at all,' said this one, 'that it is Bessas son of Phraates. Who else comes roaring in, knocks people over with playful slaps on the back, drinks half the troop's daily allowance of wine at one draft, breaks the troop commander's collarbone in a friendly wrestle, and then snores all night like seven thunderstorms?'"

Again, when beseiged with Myron in the Tower of the Snail by a band of arabs, "The giant [Bessas] was in his element, running his little battle with the smooth competence of a skilled lapidary cutting a gem."

Bessas, then, is a big, likeable man with a surperb physique and almost superhuman fighting prowess. He has faults -- he is too emotionally attached to his mother, he is impulsive, he occasionally gets into scrapes from which his companions have to extricate him. Yet these weaknesses serve to emphasize his capabilities rather than diminish them. Myron once describes Bessas thus:

> "Behold the gallant Aryan hero true,
> Of little wit and bulging thew:
> He slays a dragon or a thousand foes,
> Then trips and breaks his neck without ado!"

Bessas (a better poet than Myron) retorts:

"Here comes the sage from Hellas, grave and wise
Whose eagle gaze doth scan the starry skies;
With eyes aloft, on a cockadrill he treads,
And so concludes his heavenly surmise!"

And on the long trip to the headwaters of the Nile and back with such unexpected finds as the great red jewel from beyond the lands of Kush, it is Bessas who is the vital element of the little expedition. It is Bessas too that adds to the tale of their wanderings in such a way as to transform that tale from solid, entertaining adventure in the de Camp style to a fascinating excellence.

To write THE DRAGON OF THE ISHTAR GATE, Sprague, as always, devoted some solid research to the background and setting. In addition, he did a good bit of research on his principal character. The results are magnificent. For all his strength and agility, Bessas has that all important touch of reality -- of believability -- about him. And that ring of truth in a thoroughly heroic, bigger-than-ordinary hero makes this novel the best thing, by far, that de Camp has yet done.

Sprague has long been aware of the pitfall of making a hero too invincible. On the other hand, although he has also warned against making a hero so ordinary that the reader cares not what happens to that hero ***, Sprague has erred in the past in making many of his heroes a bit too humanly fallible.

This time, the principal character is an entirely different kind of man. In Myron are concentrated the traits common to many a de Camp type hero -- the intellectual, skeptical and reserved, is he -- but Bessas is drawn from another source.

And that source? O, come now -- a tall, broad, black-haired hero -- of bulging muscles and lightning-fast reflexes -- who goes on a quest to the lands beyond Kush and brings back a great red gem -- who is closely attached emotionally to his mother? Bessas is an affectionate picture of Robert E Howard, with a generous dash of Conan tossed in, living in an age Howard would have most enjoyed.

The result is wonderful; I unreservedly recommend it.

*** page 217ff, SCIENCE FICTION HANDBOOK, by L Sprague de Camp, Hermitage House, 1953.

############

SWACKLE
        On An Anthology
                by L Sprague de Camp
There is an outside chance (the prospects for which are looking decidedly up) that one of these days I shall be called upon to edit an anthology of short stories and novelettes in the heroic-fantasy genre. If any fellow Hyborians would offer suggestions as to what should be included, I should welcome them. For instance, with regard to well-known HF writers like Dunsany, Howard, & Leiber, is there any one special story in each case that is outstandingly better than any other by that author, or that better represents him than any other? And is there a HF writer or story, so obscure I have never heard of him or it, who or which ought to be included? If so, drop me a card. Kaor,
                L Sprague de Camp, Box 223, Wallingford, Penna

www.ingramcontent.com/pod-product-compliance
Lightning Source LLC
Chambersburg PA
CBHW080019130626
46556CB00016B/3313